Ninja School Rules

Published by Lucky Four Press, LLC, 2021
Copyright © 2021 Kim Ann / Lucky Four Press, LLC.
Library of Congress Number: 2021904929

Inquiries should be directed to: luckyfourpress@yahoo.com
or to the author at: kim@kimann.co

ISBN-13: 978-1-953774-03-3 Paperback
ISBN-13: 978-1-953774-02-6 Hardback

www.kimann.co

Ninja School Rules

Written by
Kim Ann

Illustrated by
Nejla Shojaie

Lucas looked through the doorway. This was his chance to be a ninja . . . just like his dad. But what if training was too hard? Would his dad still be proud of him?

"This is going to be so much fun!" he whispered.

Next to him, Sofia nodded. "Best way ever to spend a Saturday!"

"Good afternoon, students," the instructor yelled.

"My name is Instructor Jax, and this is Instructor Kay. When we ask a question, please answer with either 'Yes, Instructor' or 'No, Instructor.' Do you understand?"

"Yes, Instructor!" the kids yelled— all but Lucas.

Oh, no. I should have answered, too, he thought. *We haven't even started, and already I did something wrong!*

"Can anyone tell me why we respond to instructors this way?" asked Instructor Kay.

Marshall raised his hand first.
"It's a sign of respect, Instructor."

"Very good!" Instructor Jax replied. "You've just learned the first rule of being a ninja: Good Ninjas Show Respect. Besides instructors, who else should we show respect to?"

"Our parents and grandparents, Instructor!" Aleena said.

"Our teachers and friends at school, Instructor!" Asher said.

"Yes! Those are both great answers," said Instructor Jax. "Who else?"

Lucas froze as Instructor Kay's eyes fell on him. Should he answer? But what if he answered wrong?

"Lucas, what do you think?" she asked.

"Maybe people who help us?" Lucas said nervously. "Like police officers and firefighters?"

"Yes, excellent!" said Instructor Jax. "Now, who's ready to learn your first ninja move!"

All around him, Lucas saw everyone else cheering. He wanted to cheer, too, but he was nervous. What if he did the moves wrong? What if he couldn't do them at all?

"First, put both hands above your head," Instructor Jax said. "Squeeze your hands into fists, with your thumbs on the outside."

"Good," Instructor Jax said, "Now, lower your arms and place your fists one on each side of your belt, like this."

Instructor Jax put his hands on his belt, and the kids did the same.

That was easy, Lucas thought.

"We are going to toss balloons in the air," Instructor Jax said. "Keeping your hand in a tight fist, lift your arm to your forehead to block the balloons from hitting you. They should bounce right off your fist."

Lucas watched as the instructors moved across the room toward him.

Thump! Thump! Thump! One by one, his friends hit the balloons away.

Soon, it was Lucas's turn.

Instructor Jax tossed a balloon into the air and stepped back.

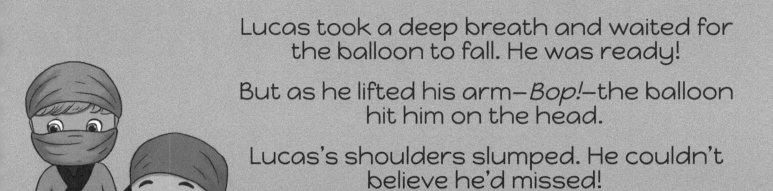

Lucas took a deep breath and waited for the balloon to fall. He was ready!

But as he lifted his arm—*Bop!*—the balloon hit him on the head.

Lucas's shoulders slumped. He couldn't believe he'd missed!

"It's okay, Lucas, you'll get another chance," Instructor Jax said, walking back to the front of the class.

"You all did very well with your eyes open," Instructor Jax continued. "Now, let's see if you can do as well with your eyes closed. Pay attention. When you think it's time, block!"

Lucas closed his eyes. All around him, he could hear the soft shuffle of feet and the *Thump! Thump! Thump!* of balloons being hit.

Suddenly, he felt something near him. *This is it!* he thought. *It must be!*

He waited until he thought the balloon was in front of him and lifted his arm. *Thump!*

"I did it!" he cheered.

"Congratulations!" Instructor Jax said.
"You just learned your first ninja move.

Instructor Jax looked around. "Lucas," he asked. "How do you think you were able to block the balloon without seeing it?"

"I listened for the sound of you walking by," Lucas replied. "Then I listened for when it was time to block."

Instructor Jax nodded. "Great! You were mindful of yourself and your surroundings. That's rule number two of being a ninja: Good Ninjas Have Focus."

"Can anyone tell me when it is important to have focus?" asked Instructor Jax.

"At basketball practice, Instructor," said Sophia.

"At school, Instructor," answered Aleena.

Asher and Marshall yelled, "At ninja class, Instructor."

"Yes!" said Instructor Jax. "Those are all great answers."

Instructor Jax smiled. "Students, are you ready for my favorite part of new ninja training?"

All together, the students shouted, "Yes, Instructor!"

Instructor Kay disappeared into a back room. A moment later, she came back with a pile of wooden boards.

Setting the pile down, she held one board tightly in front of her.

Pow! Instructor Jax punched through it.

"Whoa!" yelled Lucas. "That was awesome!"

"Ninjas, I want you to remember something," said Instructor Jax. "If ninjas don't try, they don't succeed. If they try, they might succeed. But when ninjas believe in themselves, they always succeed! That's rule number three of being a ninja: Good Ninjas Are Confident."

"So, who wants to try?" Kay asked.

Marshall and Aleena went first. *Crack! Pop!*

"May I go next, Instructor?" asked Asher. *Snap!*

Finally, it was time for Lucas and Sophia to break their boards.

"I'm not sure I can," said Lucas. "What if I miss? Or hurt my hand?"

"Remember what Instructor Jax said," Sophia told him. "When ninjas believe in themselves, they always succeed. I believe in you!"

"You're up, Lucas. You got this!" said Instructor Kay.

"Come on, Lucas. You'll do great!" said Aleena.

"Let's break together," suggested Sophia.

Lucas nodded. "Ninja confidence, just like my dad.
I can do this."

"Ready?" Asher said, "One, two, three. GO!"

Bam! Lucas's hand slammed through the board, smashing it. Beside him, he saw Sofia's broken board.

"Yes!" he shouted. "We did it!"

"Well done, Lucas and Sophia. Well done all of you," said Instructor Jax. "I'm proud of you. When a student was struggling, you came together to support them. That's rule number four of being a ninja: Good Ninjas Show Kindness. Class has ended for today, but we'll see you back here next week!"

Ninja School Rules

1. Good Ninjas Show Respect

2. Good Ninjas Have Focus

3. Good Ninjas Are Confident

4. Good Ninjas Show Kindness

As the students came together to bow out, Lucas looked back at his broken board lying on the floor and smiled. For the first time, he really felt like a ninja.

It felt great!

Meet the Ninjas

Sophia   Asher   Lucas   Aleena Marshall

Ultimate Ninjas

Katelyn Clementine Coco Noah Avelyn

Arya   Taytum   Gabriel   Braden   Bailey

Dedicated to Grandmaster Tom Vo.
Thank you for always being the best father, mentor, and role model.
For teaching me to be kind, respectful, and the best version of myself.
With love and appreciation -Tom Vo, Jr.

Featured Titles

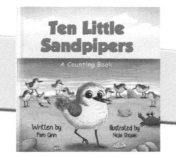

Ten Little Sandpipers

A Counting Book

Written by Kim Ann   Illustrated by Nejla Shojaie

Ninja School Rules

Written by Kim Ann   Illustrated by Nejla Shojaie

If you enjoyed this book, check out these other titles by author Kim Ann!

www.kimann.co

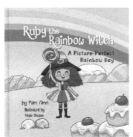

Ruby the Rainbow Witch
A Picture-Perfect Rainbow Day
by Kim Ann
Illustrated by Nejla Shojaie

Ruby the Rainbow Witch
The Lost Swirly-Whirly Wand
by Kim Ann
Illustrated by Nejla Shojaie

Ruby the Rainbow Witch
Meet the Amber Fairies
by Kim Ann   Illustrated by Nejla Shojaie

Ruby the Rainbow Witch
Let's Color
by Kim Ann   Illustrated by Nejla Shojaie

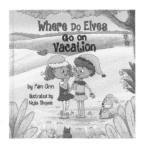

Goldy the Puppy and The Missing Socks
by Kim Ann   Illustrated by Nejla Shojaie

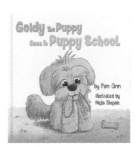

Goldy the Puppy Goes to Puppy School
by Kim Ann   Illustrated by Nejla Shojaie

Goldy the Puppy and The Birthday Spa Day
by Kim Ann   Illustrated by Nejla Shojaie

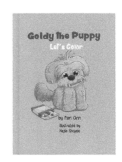

Goldy the Puppy Let's Color
by Kim Ann   Illustrated by Nejla Shojaie

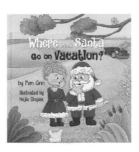

Where Do Elves Go on Vacation
by Kim Ann   Illustrated by Nejla Shojaie

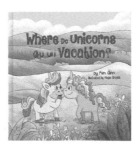

Where Does Santa Go on Vacation?
by Kim Ann   Illustrated by Nejla Shojaie

Where Do Unicorns Go on Vacation?
by Kim Ann   Illustrated by Nejla Shojaie

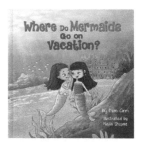

Where Do Dinosaurs Go on Vacation?
by Kim Ann   Illustrated by Nejla Shojaie

Where Do Mermaids Go on Vacation?
by Kim Ann   Illustrated by Nejla Shojaie

CPSIA information can be obtained
at www.ICGtesting.com
Printed in the USA
LVHW070316180821
695556LV00008B/168